The Magic Unicorn & Sleepy Dinosaur

Bed Time Stories Collection

Short Bedtime Stories to Help Your Children & Toddlers Sleep and Relax! Great Dinosaurs & Unicorn Fantasy Tales to Dream about all Night!

By Hannah Watson

"The Magic Unicorn & Sleepy Dinosaur Bed Time Stories Collection: Short Bedtime Stories to Help Your Children & Toddlers Sleep and Relax! Great Dinosaurs & Unicorn Fantasy Tales to Dream about all Night!" Written by "Hannah Watson".

The Magic Unicorn & Sleepy Dinosaur Bed Time Stories Collection is a bundle of the books "The Magic Unicorn – Bedtime Stories for Kids", & "The Sleepy Dinosaurs – Bedtime Stories for Kids".

Hope You Enjoy!

The Magic Unicorn

Bedtime Stories for Kids

Short Bedtime Stories to Help Your
Children & Toddlers Fall Asleep and
Relax! Great Unicorn Fantasy Stories
to Dream about all Night!

By Hannah Watson

Table of Contents

Table of Contents

Introduction

Bedtime is a time for beautiful stories and wonderful friends. Here you will discover both in the magical world of unicorns. While you read these stories, the words, and sounds will soon have your little one drifting on the clouds of eternal happiness and joy as they slip into the land of sleep.

These short stories are especially written to help your munchkin find a peaceful and contented way to enjoy a good night's rest. Peacefully drifting into an adventure with the joyful and oh-so-cute Unicorn, your child will learn beautiful skills such as friendship, love, forgiveness, and trust.

As you snuggle up together under the covers, enjoy these stories and be transported to a magical world filled with incredible friends and wonderful adventures that will lull you off to pleasant dreams and ensure a peaceful evening. Now, snuggle in and get ready to meet the Magic Unicorn.

Chapter 1: The Unicorn and Animal Friends

A Story of the Unicorn, the Frog, the Caterpillar, and the Fish

Once upon a time, the Magic Unicorn was running through the rainbow valley when she saw a brightly colored stream up ahead. In the land of magic, rainbows were everywhere, and the water soon glowed with these bright colors.

Next to the river was a frog, staring deeply into the water. The frog seemed to be searching for something, and he seemed really upset.

"What's the matter, Frog?" the unicorn asked, frowning into the water too.

"My friend the caterpillar is missing, and I think he has fallen into the water, and I can't see him anywhere." Frog's ribbit sounded.

"Well, maybe I can help you find your friend?" Unicorn offered.

"Can you swim under the water and find the caterpillar?" Frog asked, jumping up and down in excitement.

"No, no. Settle down, Frog. I can't swim, but you're a frog, so can't you swim?"

"No, I can't swim; my mommy never taught me how," Frog sadly said.

"Oh, that's okay. I know someone who can help us. He is an excellent swimmer, and I'm sure he will be able to rescue the caterpillar soon." The unicorn gently dropped her bright horn into the water, stirring the surface with the tip of her horn. She smiled happily, sending out waves of joy and friendship into the water.

Soon, a bright little body rose from deep in the river. It was a beautiful fish, who was rising up to speak to the unicorn. She had a dazzling body with blue fins and a bright red mouth that opened and spoke.

"How can I help you, Unicorn?" the fish asked, her lips opening and closing as she spoke.

"Help me find my friend the caterpillar please," asked the frog.

The fish smiled happily and dove back into the water. Being a good swimmer, the fish soon began to search everywhere for the caterpillar. But after much searching, there was still no sign of the caterpillar in the water. The agile fish swam and swam and swam, but she found no sign of the caterpillar anywhere. Frog became really worried now. What had happened to his friend the caterpillar?

The unicorn tried to comfort the frog, seeing how sad and unhappy he was. It wasn't nice to look for your friends and not find them anywhere. The unicorn was a good friend, and she stayed by Frog, gently tapping his shoulder with her great horn, showering him with waves of magical friendship and comfort. Then suddenly the unicorn laughed and called the frog's name.

"Frog, when last did you see your friend the caterpillar?" she asked with a happy smile.

"Yesterday. He was on that leaf over there..." Frog was surprised. There, under the leaf where he had last seen his friend was a beautiful new butterfly. The butterfly had wrapped his colorful wings, and he was sleeping soundly.

"Is that my friend the caterpillar?" Frog asked, and when the unicorn nodded happily, he was so relieved. His friend had been there all this time, sleeping and becoming an even more beautiful creature.

A Story of the Unicorn, the Fake Unicorn, the Bear, Lion, Eagle, and Beaver

One day, not long ago, the unicorn was happily grazing in a valley of the Magic kingdom. She was smiling and enjoying the green grass and listening to the birds sing. The sun was shining warmly on her pale coat, making her feel great.

Suddenly, the unicorn heard a loud voice, shouting angrily. It was the eagle, crying out in anger and diving down to sit near the unicorn.

"What's the matter, Eagle?" the unicorn asked, looking up in worry.

"Why did you break my nest, Unicorn?" the eagle unhappily demanded to know.

"I did not do that, Eagle." Unicorn was surprised by the eagle's words.

"I saw the markings of your horn on the tree beneath my nest. Now my nest lies broken on the ground." Eagle almost cried.

"It wasn't me, Eagle, I promise. I have been eating grass in the valley all day." Unicorn explained, but before she could continue, a great roar sounded again, and the Bear came running out of the nearby woods.

"What is the matter, Bear?" Unicorn asked in concern.

"Why did you break my home, Unicorn?" the Bear roared.

"I did not do any such thing, Bear." Unicorn was growing worried now. She had never done such a bad thing before, and she would never hurt the other creatures in the land of magic.

"But I saw your horn marking the ground around the fallen tree where I lived, and now, it is broken apart."

"Unicorn! Why did you break up my home?" Yet another roar sounded, and the Unicorn turned to see the Beaver come running from the nearby dam.

"Hello, Beaver. I didn't do that," Unicorn said, wondering what was going on.

"I saw your hoof prints in the mud near my home, and you pulled all the sticks from my home, breaking it open." Beaver was unhappy; this was ruining his day.

"Easy now, my friends. I have never harmed any of you, so why would I go and break up your homes?" Unicorn asked, stamping a hoof in frustration and softly blowing on the grass.

"Then who would do this?" the animals asked in a chorus.

"Let's find out." Unicorn winked and began to move her magical horn, drawing in the air as the diamond at the horn's tip began to glow. Soon, they saw the nearby home of the Eagle, and they also saw an animal was hiding in the trees—it was the lion. She was the one to blame. She had made everyone think that the unicorn had broken their homes, when really, Lion was the fake unicorn.

"Lion, please come here," the unicorn called, stamping her hoof again. Lion came closer, walking low, and growling unhappily. "Lion, why did you break these animals' homes?"

"I am lonely, Unicorn," the Lion said, scratching in the sand, making the same markings as the unicorn made when she ate grass.

"Lion, you don't have to do something like that because you are lonely. We'll be your friends," the unicorn offered with a smile. The lion couldn't believe her ears. She had been so mean to the other animals, but they were still willing to be her friends. With the unicorn's help, Lion made some friends, and they spent the rest of the day playing in the sunshine.

Chapter 2: The Unicorn and More Friends

The Unicorn and the Magic Rock

Early one morning, the Magic Unicorn was walking through the valley in the kingdom of Magic. She was in the mood for an adventure, and she decided that she would teach herself to fly. You see, unicorns have the power to make magic mist and then run through the air on it. This was like flying, but the unicorn needed some special skills.

All of Unicorn's other unicorn friends were able to make magic mist, but she didn't know how to make it yet. Both her parents were able to fly with the magic mist, but the unicorn didn't know how to do it herself.

So, she ran through the valley, prancing about, while she made little clouds of magic mist with her pink lips. She could make little bits of magic mist, but she couldn't make enough to lift her into the sky.

After some time, the unicorn became tired and stopped to rest by a large rock. The rock was engraved with magic words and lines, and as the unicorn stopped by the rock, it suddenly moved and rose up into the sky!

The unicorn was so surprised that she let out a small scream and a little cloud of magic mist as she jumped backwards. Looking at the rock floating in the sky before her, Unicorn decided to be brave, and she asked the rock, "Hello, who are you?"

"I am the Magic Rock," the Rock said in a loud and grumbly voice.

"I didn't know rocks can fly." The unicorn was surprised and looked at the rock with admiration.

"Of course, we can. Especially if we are Magic Rocks." The Rock gave a little twirl in the air, making the unicorn laugh with joy.

"How did you learn to fly, Mr. Magic Rock?" Unicorn asked eagerly. She hoped the rock could perhaps teach her how to fly too.

"Well, it helps to get a little push in the right direction! Ha-ha!" the Magic Rock laughed, sending a little sand tumbling from its big and round body.

"Can you please help me to learn to fly, Mr. Magic Rock?" the unicorn pleaded.

She danced on her little hooves in excitement, hoping her new friend could show her the way. Her silver mane flew through the air as she nodded her head so happily. The unicorn pawed at the ground, sending up a cloud of magic mist to try and find her ability to fly.

"Of course, I will help you, little unicorn."

"What do I need to do?" Unicorn asked, lifting her brightly glowing horn to the sky.

"You need to jump higher into the air. To do this, you need to have some help until you know how to do it." The Magic Rock floated closer to the unicorn, gesturing to the unicorn that she had to run and jump up on the Magic Rock as it floated in the air.

"Okay, I will try my best." The unicorn took a deep breath, and she ran to the Magic Rock as fast as she could. When her small hooves landed on the Magic Rock, she blew out as much of the magic mist as she could. The magic mist moved higher and higher, and soon, the little unicorn was flying through the air, carried by her magic mist.

The Unicorn and the Child in the Sunny Field

Later that afternoon, the unicorn was flying through the bright blue sky. She was laughing with joy at the clouds floating past her as she flew upon the magic mist. The world below her was so beautiful. She could see small fields in different colors below her as she flew through the sky.

Below her, she suddenly saw a bright and sunny field. The grass was a beautiful green, and the wind gently moved the long stems of grass to its breath. The unicorn suddenly saw a small child sitting in the field. Curious, the unicorn flew lower and began to land in the sunny field.

As her bright pink hooves touched down on the warm earth, she ran a few steps before stopping with a happy sigh. Turning to look at the small child in the field, she soon walked closer.

"Hello." The unicorn smiled broadly with joy. "I'm the Magic Unicorn. What's your name?"

The child looked at the unicorn with large eyes and seemed afraid. "My name is Andy. Are you really a unicorn?"

The unicorn laughed aloud, then with a bright rainbow forming at the tip of her horn, she replied, "Yes, I am a unicorn. See, I can make rainbows."

"Were you flying over the field too?" the child asked in a small voice.

"Yes. It's so much fun. I recently made friends with the Magic Rock, and with the rock's help, I learned how to fly." The unicorn was really happy today. She had learned to fly, and now, she had met a human child for the first time ever. "Are you a real human child?"

"Yes, I'm a real child. Have you never seen a child before?" the child asked, sounding surprised.

"No, never. Here in the land of Magic, only the very best and most well behaved of children come to visit. Have you been a very good child?" the unicorn asked, tapping her front hoof.

"Yes, I am a good child. I fell asleep in my bed, and then I woke up here."

"That's so wonderful!" The unicorn was really excited now. "Would you like to come fly with me over the field?"

"I don't know. Will you be going very high?" the child asked hesitantly.

"Only as high as you can dream." The unicorn smiled happily.

"Will you be flying fast?"

"Only as fast as you can dream," the unicorn assured the child.

"Okay, then I would really like to go flying with you, Unicorn." Now also excited by a new friend, the child stood up and walked to the unicorn. "How do I get on your back, unicorn? You are really tall, and I am so small."

"Just hold onto my mane, and I will bend down so you can climb up onto my back," the unicorn offered. Their plan worked well, and with a quick climb, the child was sitting on the unicorn's back. "You need to hold on tightly, my friend. We're about to fly now."

With a shout of delight, the unicorn and the child flew into the sky. The unicorn flew low over the sunny field with her new friend, and they had a lovely time together. After several minutes of flying, the child grew tired, and the unicorn landed softly, letting the child lie down in the summer grass of the sunny field.

"Can I come visit you again, Unicorn?" the child asked sleepily.

"Of course, you can, child." And they became best friends from that day on.

Chapter 3: The Unicorn and S(caring) Friends

The Unicorn and the Nighttime Shadows

It had been a busy day for the unicorn. She had made new friends, learned to fly, and made a human friend too. Feeling a little tired, the unicorn was going home to rest. The sun was beginning to set, and the land was painted in beautiful colors of red, gold, and purple. It was so lovely to see.

To get home, the unicorn had to walk through a nearby forest. At night, the forest became a little bit scary to the unicorn, and she had never walked through it so late at night before.

Stepping along the wide path, her bright pink eyes grew larger as she watched the shadows form under the trees. Her little heart beat a bit faster, and she wanted to run back to her home.

Suddenly, she saw a shadow move towards her, but it stopped a bit away from her, and she heard a small voice whisper, "Don't be afraid, Unicorn. We're not going to hurt you."

"Wh-Who are you?" the unicorn asked, her voice trembling a little.

"I am a nighttime shadow." The shadow moved a little, and then the unicorn saw the shadow unzip a headpiece, revealing a small little elf.

"You're a nighttime shadow? I thought shadows were scary!" the unicorn asked, then laughed nervously.

"We don't mean to be. You see, we are just here to take care of the trees at night, and so we dress in these shadow suits to keep warm," the elf explained. "Every time you move and make a shadow, you are helping us take care of the land."

"Oh, really?" the unicorn was surprised.

"Yes, you see, we nighttime shadows can dance while we take care of the plants and the world at night." To show the unicorn how it worked, the nighttime shadow began to dance, leap, and change into wonderful shapes.

"Can I make those shapes too?" The unicorn was no longer afraid, and she was really excited about making shadows too.

With the shadow elf's help, the unicorn made some lovely nighttime shadows. She made small unicorns running under the trees, a bird flying away with her tail, and she also made some pretty flowers by using her magic mist to make shadows.

She had such fun that she was no longer afraid of the nighttime shadows at all. After spending some time making fun shadows, the unicorn gave her new friend the nighttime shadow elf a big hug, wished them well in caring for the trees and began to walk home. She was now happy to walk in the dark forest because she knew that the shadows were just more of the special elves caring for the trees.

The Unicorn and the Spider

Early the next morning, the unicorn headed out to go play in the valleys of the magic kingdom again. She was really excited to meet some new friends today. As she walked under the trees, she suddenly heard a small voice shout, "Stop! Stop!"

Looking around, the unicorn couldn't see anyone there, so she began walking again, only to hear the shouting again, "Stop! Stop! Please don't go any further."

"Hello? Who's there?" the unicorn asked, looking around the forest.

"It's me, the spider. Please don't walk ahead. You'll break my web, which I had spent the whole night making." The unicorn looked ahead, and there, before her, was a beautiful spider's web. It hung across the pathway. The early morning dew had hung the web with bright silver lights. It was so pretty to see!

"Oh, wow! I am so sorry; I didn't mean to break your web."

The unicorn looked at the web, and finally, she saw the spider crawl along the silver lines of the web.

"Hello, my name is the Magic Unicorn. What's your name?" The unicorn sat down, letting the spider crawl closer to her. "Why are you building such a beautiful web across the path?"

"My name is Jasper. I'm a forest spider, and I build my webs to catch the sunlight at dawn. You see, my webs make lights with the dew drops, and I use the light from my webs," the spider explained. She climbed to one of the dew drops and unscrewed it, revealing that it kept on glowing.

"Wow, is that how the other animals have lights for their homes at night?" The unicorn had never stopped to think where the animals got their lights from.

"Yes, I make the lights for them. It only lasts one night, so I have to be ready at dawn to make many more lights for all of the animals." The spider began to gather the other lights into a big bag that hung from each of her eight shoulders.

"Can I help you, Jasper?" the unicorn offered, rising up.

"You are too big to pick the lights, Unicorn. However, you can help me deliver the lights when I have collected them all." Jasper the spider was really grateful for the unicorn's help. Usually, she could only carry a few bags to the animals' homes, but with the unicorn's help, she would be able to carry all of the bags and deliver them safely and quickly.

Once Jasper had collected all of the lights, she hung them from the unicorn's mane, tying them in securely. The lights shone prettily in her silver mane, and the unicorn was really happy to be helping the spider with her important work. They rushed about, and within a few short minutes, the unicorn and the spider had delivered all of the lights to the animals.

The Magic Unicorn promised to help the spider deliver the lights every morning, and that is why unicorns have such sparkly manes, from all the lights they carry.

Chapter 4: The Unicorn's Monster Friends

The Unicorn and the Zesty Zombies Meet the Savvy Skeleton and the Grinning Ghost

It was Halloween in the land of Magic. The animals were all busy dressing up in scary outfits to tease their friends. The unicorn decided to color her mane a bright red with the berries from the love tree. She believed this would make her seem like the phoenix with its burning tail.

Happily running through the valley, the Magic Unicorn enjoyed swishing her tail to let the red color of her tail glow against the sunset. The Magic Unicorn was so pleased with meeting all her friends, and she carried some special treats she had made in a bag, handing them out to all of her friends as they laughed and ran in the valley.

The Magic Unicorn was running along when she suddenly heard loud shouting from the woods. Her eyes grew large when she saw the shapes moving from the forest. She couldn't believe it, but there, before her eyes, were several zombies who came ambling out of the tree line.

Some of the animals were scared when they heard the zombies walking near. However, as soon as they came near, the Magic Unicorn could hear the laughing of her friends in their outfits. It was just for laughs!

Still giggling at the good fun her friends were having, the Magic Unicorn heard another sigh from the forest. A skeleton was walking towards them now.

"Who are you, oh, skeleton?" the unicorn asked cheerfully.

"I am a lonely skeleton, and your laughter has woken me from my sleep!" the voice sounded strange as it came from the skeleton's mouth. The Magic Unicorn began to wonder if this was also one of her friends, or if this was indeed a skeleton.

Carefully walking closer, the Magic Unicorn politely introduced herself, "Hi, I am the Magic Unicorn. Who are you?"

"I am the Savvy Skeleton. I was sleeping, and your laughter woke me up. But now, I can't find my friend, the Grinning Ghost." The skeleton stopped suddenly, causing the bony head to fall to the ground. "Oh, no, not again."

"Do you need some help, Savvy Skeleton?" The Magic Unicorn had always been a helpful creature, and she wanted to help all the animals in the Magic kingdom.

"Yes, please. I can't see where I have dropped my head. Please, can you help me pick it up?" The Savvy Skeleton quickly followed the unicorn's guidance to find his head again. Sighing happily, he placed his head back on his shoulders and asked again, "Where can I find my friend, the Grinning Ghost?"

"Where did you see him last?" the unicorn asked.

"I saw him over by the big oak tree in the middle of the valley. But my bones are so very cold now, and I don't think I can walk that far." The skeleton was clearly used to complaining.

"You can ride on my back." The Magic Unicorn was not afraid of anything, and she could see the Savvy Skeleton was not scary at all.

"Really? I haven't ridden a horse in several hundred years." The Savvy Skeleton scratched at his bony head.

"It's easy. Hop on." And off they went to the middle of the valley where the large oak tree stood. Reaching the tree, they saw a pale shape playing in the branches. It was none other than the Grinning Ghost. Once again, the Magic Unicorn had helped bring friends together, even if they were a little strange.

The Unicorn's Tea Party With the Ridiculous Rat

Early one morning, the Magic Unicorn was walking next to the river, planning on taking a swim in the nearby lake. She was in a happy mood, though this was nothing new. The unicorn was always in a happy mood. Happily skipping on the big river stones, she sang to herself and splashed into the puddles of water on the riverbank.

"Hey, stop messing around, you four-hooved nightmare!" a voice suddenly shouted at the Magic Unicorn. Surprised, she stopped in the middle of a puddle and looked around, but she could see nobody there. She pawed at the puddle in annoyance. No one dared to call her a nightmare, not even her brother!

"I said, stop it!" The voice sounded again, and looking up, the unicorn could see a small rat sitting atop a nearby rock.

"I'm sorry—"

"And well you should be!" the rat interrupted the unicorn. She didn't like this rat's attitude at all and huffed in frustration. Her mommy had always told her to treat all creatures with respect and compassion.

"What I was going to say, Mr. Rat, is that I'm sorry, but I didn't see you there." She walked closer to the rat.

"You didn't see me? I am larger than life, I am a massive creature, and I am a loud creature. How could you not see me?" The rat seemed to be really upset and was almost bouncing on the rock in anger.

"Be calm, Mr. Rat. I meant no offense." The unicorn was not sure why this rat was so angry at her.

"Yes, it's just typical. No one sees me, so no one visits me. Humph!" the rat complained, hopping off the rock and walking away.

"Mr. Rat, is it true no one visits you?" The unicorn felt sorry for the rat, and she walked after him, quickly catching up to him.

"No one comes for tea, and no one eats my delicious scones!" the rat moaned.

"May I come for tea, Mr. Rat?" the unicorn politely asked.

The rat stopped, then spun around on his scrawny legs. "Really?" He scurried up the unicorn's leg and pulled her ear open, asking again in an excited tone, "Really! Do you really want to come for tea?"

"Sure. I would love to have tea with you." The unicorn gently shook the rat from her ear.

"Oh, splendid! Wonderful! Most excellent! We shall have a tea party for just the two of us." The rat was being quite ridiculous and over the top, but the unicorn decided to smile and join in the game, wanting to cheer up the lonely rat.

"Sure, it's a grand plan." The rat scurried around, seeming to run in circles as he set out his finest cups and prepared some tea. He also had some elderflower scones, which he had made the previous night, and he served these up with golden daisy creme. It proved to be a delicious feast for the unicorn, though she had to be careful not to break the cups with her great mouth. The ridiculous rat turned out to be a wonderful host, and they had a lovely morning on the riverbank, sipping tea and eating scones.

The Unicorn Meets the Devilish Dragon and the Misunderstood Medusa

As the unicorn grew older, she became more and more adventurous, and since she could fly really well now, she also began to travel much further from home. One morning, she decided to fly out over the crystal ocean that was nearby the magic valley. She had always been interested in the sea-gulls who gathered on the rocks at the ocean's edge.

Her lungs were so big and strong now, and she could make lots of magic mist and fly really far. When she grew a little tired, she flew down to a nearby island to rest. She had never been here before, and she had barely landed when she saw a great big dragon walk out from a nearby cave. He huffed and he puffed, and he blew out a cloud of fire. The Magic Unicorn became a bit afraid, but she believed in standing her ground, and she pawed at the ground, but asked in a soft voice, "Who are you, Mr. Dragon?"

"I am the Devilish Dragon, and you are trespassing on my island." The dragon huffed again, preparing to spit out more flames. Of course, being a magical creature, the Magic Unicorn was immune to dragon fire. She was quite safe, and she had known from the first puff of flames that she was safe.

"I am only resting for a few minutes, Devilish Dragon. There is no need to be angry." The Magic Unicorn prepared to make some magic mist to carry her away from this grumpy dragon.

"Oh, wait. Please, don't go," the dragon suddenly pleaded. "I didn't realize you can fly. Please may I ask a big favor of you?" The dragon sat down then, and the Magic Unicorn could see the dragon had a broken wing.

"What happened to your wing, Devilish Dragon?" the unicorn asked gently.

"I broke it in a big storm many months ago. Now, I can never leave this island again."

"I would carry you, Mr. Dragon, but I am afraid you are too big for me to carry." The unicorn felt sorry for the dragon, and she could now understand how sad the dragon must feel to be on this island all alone.

"No, that's okay, Unicorn. I don't need to leave this island. It's actually quite nice here. I am only lonely because I don't have any way to let my wife, Medusa, know I am here." The dragon sighed, and two columns of smoke rose from its nose.

"Where is Medusa? Perhaps I can take a message to her, or even bring her here?" The Magic Unicorn knew love was the most powerful magic on earth, and perhaps when Medusa came here, she could help the dragon heal his wing.

"She is on an island not far from here." The dragon quickly gave the unicorn directions, and she hopped off into the air, flying to the island as fast as she could make magic mist.

Medusa was not happy to see the unicorn, and she was a fearsome woman to make unhappy. Her hair was made up of many snakes, each of which had two long teeth. But the unicorn was brave, and she easily kept out of reach of the snakes until she could deliver the dragon's message. Then Medusa became calm, and her snakes went to sleep.

"Do you mean to tell me my husband, the dragon, is on an island nearby?" she asked, sounding sad.

"Yes, and he misses you terribly. Come, Medusa, climb on my back, and I will take you to him."

"I had believed he had left me. He has been gone for so many months now. Fearing for him, I have been quite angry and mean to everyone who comes near me." Medusa began to cry.

"It's okay, Medusa. You were worried about the dragon, and you were simply misunderstood," the unicorn comforted her.

Sniffing, Medusa climbed onto the Magic Unicorn's back, and they flew back to the dragon as quickly as possible. Medusa happily embraced the dragon, and they walked into his cave with a fond wave to the Magic Unicorn. Again, the unicorn had managed to save the day and help reunite the grumpy Devilish Dragon with his wife, the Misunderstood Medusa.

Chapter 5: The Unicorn's Mythical Encounters

The Unicorn, the Fairy, and the Troll Meet the Will-o'-Wisp

Tonight is a special event. The Magic Unicorn's friends, the fairy and the troll, are off on an adventure. They have decided to have a midnight picnic in the forest. The spider was kind enough to give them a few of the dew lights that are made by the web. They were prepared, and they had packed a whole basket filled with lovely treats and games to keep themselves busy with.

The troll carried the big basket filled with treats, and the fairy rode on the unicorn's back–sitting on their picnic blanket, holding the bag of lights in place. Their parents all knew where the three youngsters were off to, and they had promised to be back before midnight.

Reaching a clearing in the forest, the youngsters set to work making the space special and beautiful for their picnic. The fairy stood on the unicorn's back, and she decorated the low hanging branches with the dew lights, while the troll dragged some of the fallen trees out of the way and spread their large blanket. Together, they began to unpack their plates and cups, and all of the lovely treats they were going to enjoy tonight.

They had brought games too. There was a blindfold so they could play hide and seek, and there was a game of pin the tail on the donkey, though Unicorn didn't really like this game very much. Soon, the clearing was ringing with the laughter of the three friends as they ate, played, and sang songs.

The basket contained lovely treats for them to enjoy. There were fresh flowers and hay pies for the unicorn, and honey cups for the fairy to drink as well as mushroom slices to eat. The troll's mommy had packed him fresh tree bark sandwiches and dried worms as a snack. Each of the friends had their own tastes, but they still enjoyed eating together.

When their bellies were full, and they had played all the games they could, they laid back on the blanket, resting their bodies and enjoying the feeling of close friendship. The unicorn had folded her legs in under her body, lying comfortably on the blanket. Troll lay next to her with his head resting on her shoulder, while the fairy had curled herself up in the unicorn's mane to have a little nap.

Unicorn suddenly looked off into the night, snorting in surprise. "What is that over there?"

"What?"

"In the forest. That light." The unicorn knew there were no creatures living in this part of the forest. A bright green light was moving towards them through the dark forest. It moved in a strange way, rolling and turning through the trees. "Is it a will-o'-wisp?" Unicorn was afraid now.

The will-o'-wisp wasn't something she was familiar with, but she had heard stories. Troll jumped to his feet, ready to protect his friends, while the unicorn also stamped her feet and stood behind him. The light drew nearer and nearer and nearer. Then it stopped, and they were amazed to see the light was not one light but many smaller lights. Curious, the friends looked closer, and the unicorn called out, "Hello? Who is out there?"

Several small voices responded, "Hello, we're the firefly family. May we please come and join you on your picnic?"

"Certainly. But why are you flying so strangely and glowing like a will-o'-wisp?" Troll asked, blinking his eyes as they came closer.

"We are afraid of the dark, so we blink our lights to look scary to protect ourselves." The fireflies blinked their lights happily as they entered the clearing.

"Would you like some treats? We still have some left," the unicorn offered, settling down again. They visited with the fireflies for a while, then they headed home, not wanting to keep their parents waiting. Fairy was still asleep in the unicorn's mane, and while the troll carried their basket, they left the dew lights behind so the fireflies would have more light and not be afraid any longer.

24

Chapter 6: The Unicorn's Colorful Friends

Brindle and the Rainbow Unicorns

The Magic Unicorn was so excited! Her family was going to a unicorn family reunion. She would meet all of her cousins and nieces and nephews, not to mention her uncles and aunts and grandfathers and grandmothers. Many of them she hadn't seen for a long time. She was really looking forward to seeing them all again.

The reunion was going to take place at the beach of the crystal sea. Different members of her family were traveling from all over the land to be there, and for three days, they would spend time together, hold races, and enjoy lovely family feasts.

Arriving at the beach, the Magic Unicorn looked at all the strange faces for a while, then recognizing different cousins and aunts and uncles, she felt more at ease. Greeting them all with a unicorn embrace, she felt warm and loved. A unicorn embrace was when two unicorns touched their horn tips together and then hugged their long necks around each other. They might even place a kiss on each other's shoulders or back, like a mother unicorn grooms her baby.

The Magic Unicorn suddenly felt a tug at her mane, and looking down, she saw a small unicorn standing next to her. This unicorn was so small, she was barely a pony, and she was a mixture of colors, which was most unusual for a unicorn. She had stripes of blue, orange, red, yellow, green, and purple all over her body.

"Hello, my name is Brindle," the unicorn shyly introduced herself. "I'm your niece."

"Nice to meet you, Brindle. My, what lovely colors you have in your coat!" The Magic Unicorn complimented her small niece.

"Thank you. My mommy and my daddy are different colors, so I am all of their families' colors." Brindle smiled bashfully and lowered her head.

"That's lovely, Brindle. I have never met a unicorn like you before." With her new niece at her side, the Magic Unicorn set off to meet the rest of their family members.

While the Magic Unicorn and Brindle chatted happily, they soon realized the other unicorns looked at Brindle strangely, choosing to walk away. This saddened Brindle, and the Magic Unicorn didn't know how to comfort her small niece.

"You should go play with the other unicorns. They don't like my colors, so I'll go play alone." Brindle didn't want the Magic Unicorn to miss out on being with the rest of their family because of her. Hanging her head, she walked off towards the waves, sat down and watched the water make surf and wash up on the beach.

The Magic Unicorn was very upset. She thought and thought of a way to make everyone see how Brindle was also part of their family. Finally, she had an idea. Turning, she ran into the nearby hills as fast as she could. She needed the help of some friends. The bees could help with pollen for yellow, grass stains for green, flower sap for blue and purple, and mud for red.

The unicorns were all gathered together to have some races when they suddenly stopped and snorted in surprise. The Magic Unicorn came walking in with Brindle at her side. She had colored her lovely silver coat with all the colors of the rainbow so Brindle wouldn't be alone. The two brindle unicorns were smiling happily, and they walked up to the rest of their family laughing with joy. Soon the other unicorns were laughing too, and before long, they were all coloring their coats with different colors and became rainbow unicorns together. Brindle was no longer alone.

Brindle and the Day of Color

There comes a day in every unicorn's life when they get to choose the color of their mane and tail. Though they may be born with a white or a brown tail and mane, they can choose on this day if they want to keep this color or rather accept another color. It is only on this day, which comes once in their lives, that they can choose their colors. It is known as the Day of Color.

While at the family reunion, both Brindle and the Magic Unicorn would celebrate their Day of Color. It was a huge day for the whole of the unicorn family. They planned games, prepared special food, and each unicorn family member offered advice to the two unicorns on which color to choose.

Red manes and tails were known to mean the unicorn was a fast runner, while white manes and tales were associated with wisdom. Choosing black as the color of your mane or tail would mean you were a proud fighter, while brown was said to be the color of peace. Silver manes and tails were associated with kindness and joy, while gold colored manes and tails were said to be a sign of nobility. There were so many colors to choose from, and both the young unicorns didn't know which colors to choose.

It was said the unicorns had to choose a color representing some part of who they are. If they were known to be friendly, they would usually choose brown or silver. Those unicorns who ran all day would naturally choose red, while the brave unicorns who kept the land safe would choose black. But what would they do when they were known for all of these?

The Magic Unicorn was known for being kind, friendly, wise, and brave. She had saved her friends, helped them when in need, ran like the wind, and she could fly really well too. Which color would be best for her then? What do you think?

Brindle, her unicorn niece, was known for being kind, shy, and friendly. While she didn't make friends easily, she had won the hearts of her family with the help of the Magic Unicorn.

Finally, the moment of their choosing had come. Which colors would they choose? Brindle and the Magic Unicorn looked at each other, and their eyes were large as they thought of each color. Brown, black, white, gold, silver, and red—each color was so special.

Then, smiling at each other, they nodded and concentrated really hard. They both imagined the colors their manes and tails would be, and then, as everyone watched, their tails and manes glowed and shimmered. A bright light surrounded the two unicorns, and when it faded, they smiled and looked at the rest of their families who all called out in approval, stamping their hooves and neighing happily.

The two friends had chosen well, and their manes and tails were not black, not brown, not white or silver, nor were they gold or red; instead, their manes and tails were bright rainbow colors, for the two unicorns were brave and wise, kind and fast, and they were peaceful and noble. They were now real rainbow unicorns, and they celebrated with many colored manes and tails.

Chapter 7: More Unicorn Tales

The Unicorn and the Sad Child

The Magic Unicorn was walking along the road through the valley of sleep, and she proudly shook her rainbow-colored mane and tail, enjoying the sun and feeling so happy with her new colors. Suddenly, she heard a very sad cry from up ahead. Worried that someone had been hurt, she ran ahead along the road.

At the side of the road, she saw a small child sitting, crying very sadly. Stopping next to the child, the Magic Unicorn stopped and gently sniffed at the crying child.

"Hi, little child. Why are you so sad?" she asked in her soft voice.

The child rubbed her eyes and sniffed loudly, wiping away her tears before replying in a sad voice, "I am so sad because I can't fall asleep."

"You can't fall asleep?" The unicorn was surprised and sat down next to the child. "But this is the valley of sleep, and it is where all children come when they sleep."

Sadly, the child began to cry again. "I can't fall asleep. My mommy has read me stories, and my daddy has brought me a glass of warm milk, but I still can't sleep."

"Oh, I see." The Magic Unicorn thought and thought of a way to help the sad child fall asleep. Finally, she smiled widely and nodded her head in joy. She had a plan for making the child fall asleep. "I have a plan, my dear child."

"What Unicorn? Please can you help me fall asleep?" The child looked at the silver unicorn with the rainbow mane and tail with hopeful eyes.

"Climb onto my back, and I will carry you through the valley while I sing you a lullaby." The unicorn lifted her leg to allow the child to climb onto her back.

"You won't drop me, will you?" the child asked, a little worried.

"Never. Have no fear; my back is the safest place to be."

And so, the Magic Unicorn began to walk along the valley road, gently swaying her back and singing a lullaby to the sad child. Her voice was soft and soothing. She sang of the warm sun, the wide valley, and of all the friends she had made in the land of magic.

Soon the sad child was no longer sad, and she began to laugh and sing with the unicorn. Sitting on the unicorn's wide back, gently swinging along to the songs, the child became very sleepy. Her eyes grew heavy, and she lay forward across the unicorn's strong back. Sighing happily, she closed her eyes, and soon, she began to drift into sleep. Finally, the child began to dream of unicorns, rainbows, and many, many happy songs in the valley of sleep.

The Unicorn and Her Special Day

Today is going to be a very special day. The Magic Unicorn has been such a good friend, a wise creature, and a brave soul that she is going to be rewarded by the animals in the land of Magic. They have planned a ceremony to thank the unicorn for being such a sweet creature.

Everyone has been invited: the frog, the caterpillar, who is now a brightly colored butterfly, and even the fish is there, safely held in a water bowl of spider webbing. The bear, lion, beaver, and eagle are also there, hugging each other since they have become best friends with the Magic Unicorn's help.

Even the Magic Rock has hovered over, with the child who went flying with the unicorn sitting on it with a happy smile. The nighttime shadows, who were actually elves, had removed their dark costumes, and they were now dressed in bright flower shapes.

With the help of the spider, the area where they would hold the thank you party had been decorated with spider webs, which each contained flowers and dew lights of every color imaginable.

The youngsters in their zombie outfits were playing with the Savvy Skeleton and his friend, the Grinning Ghost. Even the ridiculous rat had shown up with cups of tea in his hands. Having healed his broken wing, the Devilish Dragon and his wife, the

Misunderstood Medusa, had also flown in from their island to celebrate the Magic Unicorn's special day.

Bright lights of the will-o'-wisp, the troll, and the fairy also showed up, jumping around with joy. Brindle had also come to visit with the Magic Unicorn, and she was happily showing off her multi-colored skin and hair. Even the sad child had come for a visit before enjoying another night of peaceful sleep.

All of the Magic Unicorn's friends were gathered together, and they were ready to celebrate. The only creature missing was the Magic Unicorn herself. The creatures all looked around, calling out to the unicorn to come and join them, but there was no answer. Where could she be?

The animals had all made a special necklace for the Magic Unicorn out of wild flowers and spider web, and they were so eager to help her put it on, but she was nowhere to be found.

Finally, walking through the valley of sleep, they saw the Magic Unicorn sitting with a child, both of them fast asleep. The animals smiled and gathered around the pair. The Magic Unicorn was once again helping another child get to sleep, and having been so busy herself, she was now tired and had also fallen asleep.

Gently, whispering in her ears, the animals and creatures of the land of Magic thanked the unicorn and left the beautiful flower necklace around her neck. They knew she would enjoy her sleep, and once she awoke, they could all have a feast together in the land of magic and sleep.

Afterword

So, this is it, for now. The Magic Unicorn has guided you on many beautiful stories into sleep, and we hope you will enjoy many more. Don't be surprised if your wee-one demands you to read the stories of the Magic Unicorn many more times to them as they also drift off into the land of magic and sleep.

These are memories they will cherish—these priceless nights of listening to your voice, snuggling in your arms, and joining adventures with the Magic Unicorn. Turn a page and enjoy many nights of blessed dreams and peace.

The Sleepy Dinosaurs – Bedtime Stories for Kids

Short Bedtime Stories to Help Your Children & Toddlers Fall Asleep and Relax! Great Dinosaur Fantasy Stories to Dream about all Night!

Hannah Watson

Table of Contents

Table of Contents

The Sleepy Dinosaurs and the Lonely Bird

Long ago, in a beautiful green land there were two friendly dinosaurs. They're names were Trica and Stego. These dinosaurs were always sleepy because they were always having adventures. Everyone in the land knew them as the sleepy dinosaurs.

Trica had 3 horns, two on her forehead and one on her nose, with a beautiful shield-like crown on top of her head, while Stego had spikes going from the top of his head all the way down to the tip of his tail.

One day Trica and Stego were on one of their adventures, walking through the forest to get some food. They heard a soft cry just on the other side of some bushes. They were always trying to help others around them, especially if someone was sad. So, they went to see who was crying.

They walked through to the other side of the bushes and they saw a little brown bird sitting all alone and crying.

"Hello little bird, are you okay?" Trica asked the small bird.

Stego stepped forward and introduced himself and his friend, "My name is Stego and this is Trica, is there anything we can do to help?"

"Hello," the bird spoke while sniffing. "My name is Donny and I'm very sad."

"Why are you sad?" asked Trica.

"My friends and I all grew up in the nests behind the bush here." The small bird explained while he cried. "We always loved playing together, but yesterday everything changed. My friends learned how to fly, but I didn't. I'm sad because I don't know if I'll be able to fly and play with all the other birds again." Donny paused to wipe away some tears and then continued, "I don't think I'll ever see my friends again."

The two sleepy dinosaurs looked up and saw many colorful birds flying in the sky above them. They were laughing and singing the sweet song birds sing when they are happy.

Trica and Stego felt bad for little Donny. Trica and Stego wanted to help the little bird, but they didn't know where to start. They thought they could teach him to fly, but neither one of them knew how to fly themselves. At first they weren't sure how to help, but then Trica had a great idea.

"Donny!" Trica jumped up with a big smile on her face, "Why don't you just ask your friends if they can come and play on the ground with you?" Trica suggested, excitedly.

"Yes!" Stego jumped for joy while he spoke. "I'm sure they miss you and just can't hear how sad you are from all the way up there."

"I never thought of that." Donny spoke with hope in his voice and wiped the tears he'd cried off of his face. "Maybe if I call to them, they'll hear me and come down!"

Donny jumped up off the floor and climbed up onto Trica's head. He called out to his friends with his tweets and chirps.

The sleepy dinosaurs watched as all the little birds in the sky stopped to look down when they heard Donny's voice. One by one they swooped down to the ground and the next thing Trica, Stego, and Donny could hear was the sound of birds chirping as they flew in circles around them.

"Donny, Donny, Donny!" Cheered all the little birds at once.

"Who are your new friends?" asked one of the little birds as he tilted his head with curiosity.

"Hello everyone, I missed you so much!" Donny sang as he leaped from side to side. "This is Trica and Stego. They found me here all alone and wanted to help me." Donny said, feeling thankful for the sleepy dinosaurs.

"What are you still doing down here?" One of the little blue birds asked.

"We've been looking for you Donny, we missed you!" Added a little red and black bird with excitement.

"Where did you go?"

The birds asked many questions, but Donny was just happy to hear his friends' voices again. He was happy to know that his friends missed him. They didn't even know that he was stranded here on the ground. Donny was feeling lucky to be with his friends again.

"Why did you stay down here Donny?" The red and black bird asked.

Donny felt sad again and didn't want to tell his friends that he couldn't fly like them. He didn't know how to tell them. Stego saw how embarrassed Donny was feeling and this was something Stego could help with. Stego walked forward and spoke loudly so all the birds could hear him.

"Donny would love to come and fly with you all in the sky and play with you, but he is still learning how and could use some help." Stego paused as all the birds looked at each other with shocked faces. "I'm sure you all miss Donny and you all fly so beautifully. You could teach him and then he can join you in the sky."

The birds looked at one another and chirped softly. Eventually one bird spoke up, "I don't know how to teach you, but I can try!" The bird smiled at Donny.

"I'll help too!" Said another bird, and then another, and another. Until all the birds around them were singing with excitement.

"Come on Donny." Said the birds as a few of them started to lift Donny up off of Trica's head.

They carried him to a nearby tree branch that was not high off the ground, but it was high enough to scare Donny. He was afraid to fall. The little birds gently set Donny down at the edge of the branch as Trica and Stego watched and cheered from below.

The little birds showed Donny everything they knew, and told him all they could think of to help him learn. All Donny needed to do was take a leap of faith and fly. He looked down at the ground and backed away in fear. Stego and Trica saw that he was scared and they knew what to do.

"Donny, you can do it, don't be afraid. We believe in you!" Stego yelled up to him.

"Yeah, we know you can do it, but if you do fall, we'll be right here to catch you!" Trica added. "You need to believe in yourself. If you believe you can do it, then you can. You can't let the fear of falling stop you from trying to fly."

Donny felt so happy he had such good friends. He was still afraid, but now that his friends were there to help him, he knew he could do it. He stepped forward to the very edge of the branch, spread his wings, closed his eyes, and jumped. He flapped his wings and for a moment it felt like he was falling.

He heard his friends cheering around him. Donny opened his eyes and saw that he wasn't falling but he was soaring through the sky. He flew round and round as all the birds, Trica, and Stego cheered for him.

He dived down to say farewell to Trica and Stego before going off on his new adventure.

"Thank you, for helping me. I will never forget you Stego and Trica. You taught me to try even though I was afraid." Donny shed a tear of happiness as he said goodbye.

"We will never forget you either Donny. Promise us you'll never forget this! You may learn slower than your friends do, but that doesn't mean you will never learn." Stego told him.

Donny smiled down at the sleepy dinosaurs one last time before his friends joined him in the sky. One by one they flew up into the sky. Donny joined them in their big adventure in the blue sky and finally played with them again.

"Well, I don't know about you Stego but I'm pretty sleepy after that adventure." said Trica while yawning.

"I sure am too, let's go home before mom and dad wonder where we are."

The two sleepy dinosaurs walked back home and went straight to bed. They dreamed of what tomorrow's adventure would be.

The Sleepy Dinosaurs and the Unhealthy Mice

On a warm, sunny day Trica and Stego went out to look for some healthy food to eat. They loved to eat all kinds of healthy foods, like fruits and vegetables, and all the green leaves they could find. Trica and Stego were still young, growing dinosaurs. Their parents always told them it's important to eat healthy so they can grow big and strong.

"My mom says it gives your body the energy it needs to keep you nice and strong on your adventures," Stego told Trica as they walked through the forest.

"My dad says it helps to keep your brain sharp for solving problems, and a nice healthy meal before bed always helps you go to sleep easy." Trica sang as she skipped through the bushes.

They loved to eat all kinds of fruits and vegetables, but they did have they're favorites. Trica loved to eat strawberries most of all. Stego had his own favorites too, he loved to eat lettuce the most.

As they were walking through the forest Stego wanted to have a little fun! He started to speed up and run ahead.

He yelled back to Trica, "Race you! Last one to the river is a slow egg."

"Hey! No fair, you got a head start!" Trica shouted as she started to run after Stego to catch up. "I don't want to be a slow egg again."

They ran and ran, until they finally made it to the beautiful blue river. They loved to come to the river because they could find their favorite foods there.

Just before she reached the water, Trica slipped on a rock and fell down. She wasn't hurt, but she was surprised that she had fallen. Maybe she wasn't a slow egg, but a clumsy one instead. As she got up she saw a bush full of strawberries by the side of the lake.

"Trica are you okay?" Stago asked as he ran to check on her.

"I'm okay, I just fell." Trica assured him. "Look Stego! There are strawberries!" Trica was jumping with joy as she continued, "Isn't it amazing?"

"It is! Let's go get them." Stego said as they walked toward the bush. "I hope I find some lettuce."

When they arrived at the bush they saw that the strawberries were too far back in the bush and their heads were too big to fit in there and get them. They weren't sure how they were going to get the strawberries. Just then they heard soft whispers coming from the bottom of the bush.

Stego looked a little closer, curious as to what was making the sound. He saw little whiskers sticking out from the bottom of the bush.

"Hello, who's in there?" Stego asked softly.

"He-he-hello there." Replied a tiny voice that sounded a little scared.

"My name is Stego and this is Trica." Stego greeted the tiny voice.

"You can come out if you want," Trica told them. "We're friendly and would like to meet you."

There was silence for a while and then the tiny voice replied, "Okay, we'll come out."

They watched as several small, furry, creatures with long tails ran out from underneath the bush. It was a large family of mice.

"Hello there!" All the mice spoke at once. "What are you two doing around the bush?"

Stego and Trica looked at each other, deciding to tell the mice their plan to eat the strawberries in the bush. The mice might want to eat some as well. They loved to share and maybe the mice could even help them get strawberries they couldn't reach.

"We were trying to get some strawberries from the bush to eat." Stego explained. "It's one of my friend's favorite foods. Could help us reach the ones deep inside the bush? Then we can all share."

The mice looked at each other confused.

"Why would you want to eat those things when you can have all the fatty nuts, sweet tree sap, and honey?" The mice asked at once.

"We like to eat that stuff too, but you can't eat it all the time." Trica tried to explain to the mice. "Stuff like that should be saved as a special treat, for when you've earned a reward."

"Yeah, if you always eat sugary, sweet, and fatty foods you'll become unhealthy." Stego added. "Our parents told us to keep a balanced diet. It's important to eat enough healthy food every day to help your body grow big and strong." Stego said happily.

The mice were confused because they had never heard anything like this before.

"Don't the strawberries taste bad?" One of the mice asked.

"No!" Trica replied. "Have any of you actually tasted a strawberry?"

The two dinosaurs waited for a reply. All the mice shook their heads to say no.

"If you haven't tried it, how do you know you don't like it?" Trica asked while giggling.

"Let's all work together to get the strawberries from deep inside the bush and then you can try some!" Stego suggested.

The mice agreed and decided to help. Trica used the horn on the tip of her nose and Stego used the spikes at the tip of his tail to part the bush's leaves. They held the leaves apart as the mice ran in and out of the bush. They each grabbed a strawberry and ran out to drop it on the ground. They did this many times until there was enough for everyone. The mice rushed out of the bush and Trica and Stego let go of the leaves.

They all sat down and ate the strawberries together. Trica was so happy she couldn't contain herself. All the little mice were surprised at how tasty the strawberries were. They ate until they were too full to eat anymore.

"I can't believe how sweet and juicy this strawberry is!" Said one of the mice.

"Yeah, this is so good. I think it's my new favorite." Said another.

"Well, it's certainly mine!" Trica laughed as she ate some more.

"You guys should remember that healthy food can be tasty too!" Stego said as he finished the last of his strawberries.

After they all finished, they had so much energy, they played and ran all around the lake. They ran and played all day, until it got dark. Trica and Stego yawned. They said goodbye to their new friends and thanked them for the strawberries. The two sleepy dinosaurs walked back home and went straight to bed. They dreamed of what tomorrow's adventure would be.

The Sleepy Dinosaurs and the Sharing Squirrel

It was a beautiful day. The sun was shining and there was a nice cool breeze. Trica and Stego were going to enjoy the warm weather as much as possible before winter came. They were not sure exactly when the cold months were coming, but they knew they were near.

"Trica, what should we do today?" Stego asked as they walked through the forest.

"I'm not sure, maybe we could find some berries to pick in the meadow and go play hide and seek." Trica said excitedly.

"That sounds fun!" Stego said as he jumped with joy. "Where should we go to play hide and seek?"

"We can't play in the meadow because there's nowhere for us to hide. The grass is too short and we're too big." Trica said.

"I know!" Stego shouted with excitement. "We could go to the thick part of the forest where the trees are really old, and big. We can hide behind those trees easily."

"You're right! There's also a bunch of boulders all around those woods for us to hide behind too." Trica said as she started to race off to the meadow.

Stego ran after her. They ran all the way to the meadow to pick some berries and had a wonderful time. They were so happy and energized after eating that they went straight to the deep part of the forest.

Just as they entered the deep part of the forest, Stego thought to himself that he wanted to hide first. He didn't like seeking because he wasn't good at it. He decided to challenge Trica to a race.

"Trica, let's race right to the middle of the large trees and the last one there has to seek."

"Okay Stego, You're on!" Trica happily accepted the challenge.

Trica wasn't as fast a runner as Stego, but she didn't mind getting there last. Just like Stego liked to hide, Trica liked to seek.

The race began and they ran until they came to the middle of the big trees. Stego made it to the trees before Trica. They knew they were in the middle because the biggest tree of them all was there.

They came to the big bark of the tree when Trica said, "Alright, I'm going to count from one to ten. You go hide." She closed her eyes and started to count.

Stego quickly but quietly snuck away to hide from Trica. He ran to the farthest tree he could find and hid behind it. Trica counted to ten and opened her eyes.

"Ready or not, here I come!" Trica yelled as she began her search for Stego.

She heard some rustling nearby. She thought it must be Stego. She snuck around the tree she heard the rustling behind. She didn't find Stego, instead she found a fury, little creature, with long, funny teeth, and a fuzzy tail.

She didn't want to scare the little creature, so she spoke softly with a smile on her face. "Hello there little guy, my name is Trica. I'm playing hide and seek with my friend, have you seen him?"

The animal spun around quickly and looked up at Trica. It had a huge smile on its face and its fuzzy tail danced around wildly.

"Hi, hi, hi!" The creature spoke loudly. "I'm Samantha. I'm a Saber-toothed Squirrel. Me and my friend are looking for nuts for the winter." Suddenly another fury face popped out right beside the little squirrel.

"Hi! My name is Skippy!" The second squirrel said loudly.

Trica couldn't help but giggle at them. "Why are you looking for food for winter?" Trica asked them, for this was something she didn't do herself.

"The winter is too cold for us and we don't like coming outside," Samantha explained. "We take a long nap inside our warm homes during the cold months. So we like to have enough food saved up to eat."

"That way we don't have to go out looking for food when it's cold," Skippy added.

"The problem is we can't find any food. The other squirrel in the big tree has food to feed at least five for the winter. When we asked if he would share, he said no." Samantha frowned.

"That's awful!" Trica gasped. "Let's go and find my friend Stego. Then we can both find a way to help you."

Trica and the two squirrels found Stego hiding behind a tree. Trica explained the squirrels' problem to him and then they made their way to the big tree to speak with the other squirrel. Trica and Stego were hoping they could convince him to share his food with their new friends.

As they came to the tree, they saw a chubby squirrel laying on a pile of acorns, nuts, and berries inside a large hole in the bark.

"Hello there," Trica called up to the squirrel. "May we speak with you?"

"My name is Stego and this is Trica." Stego called up as well. "We just wanted to ask you kindly if you would please share your food with these poor squirrels this winter." Stego asked politely.

The fat squirrel looked down at them with a frown and said, "No!"

Skippy and Samantha gasped at how rude he was to the dinosaurs.

"Why should I share my food?" The squirrel asked. "I worked hard to find this food. It's mine!"

Trica sighed. The squirrel made her angry but she was determined to help her new friends.

"I understand how you feel," Trica spoke kindly. "You worked hard for all this food, but even when you saw you had enough, you looked for more food. You found all the food and left none behind for the other animals. Now these little squirrels can't find any food for themselves. You have more than enough food to share."

The squirrel thought long and hard about this. He looked down at the two squirrels and saw that they were small and skinny, and he was big and fat. He looked at the pile of food he was sitting on and sighed.

"I will share my food with you." He agreed. "I see now it was wrong to gather more food than I needed. I will give you the food you need for the winter."

Skippy and Samantha jumped up and shouted, "Thank you!"

"Yes, you are a very kind squirrel," Trica told him. "Stego, we never got to playing our hide and seek game!

"No, we didn't," Stego agreed and turned to the little squirrels. "Would you like to join us?"

The squirrels jumped in excitement, even the fat one wanted to play. They all played many games with each other until the sun went down. When it got dark, Stego and Trica said goodbye to their new friends. The squirrel shared his food with Skippy and Samantha and they went home too.

The two sleepy dinosaurs walked back home and went straight to bed. They dreamed of what tomorrow's adventure would be.

The Sleepy Dinosaurs and the New Dinosaur

Trica and Stego were running through a field of flowers one beautiful morning. They were collecting as much food as they could find for the big day ahead.

"I'm so excited to see all our friends." Stego said happily as he and Trica looked for something to carry the food they had picked.

Trica and Stego were excited for the big day. They planned to have a big picnic that day. They were going to collect all their favorite foods and treats, and then make their way to the meadow. This is where they had invited all their new friends to join them.

"Yes, I am so excited! I hope they all can make it." Trica said as she pulled a giant leaf from a tree nearby. "How about this to carry the food Stego?"

"That looks perfect Trica, nice job!" Said Stego impressed at his friend's giant leaf.

They had invited all their friends to the picnic. The little birds, the adorable mice, the kind squirrels, and all kinds of creatures through the land they had met on their adventures.

They found a giant leaf to carry the food and searched for their favorite foods. They knew a lot of their friends loved the healthy food that Stego and Trica brought them to eat. The two dinosaurs knew exactly where to go to look for these treats. They had to make sure to get enough food to feed everyone, so they tried to pack extra just in case.

They had nearly come to the end of their search for food. They found a lot of food and were happy with their hard work. They had found all kinds of berries, apples, broccoli, pears, lettuce, and more. The giant leaf was almost full of food. It was almost too heavy for the two dinosaurs to drag, but they managed.

"We have a lot of food," Stego said to Trica.

"Yes, but we still need to find some oranges. They are so juicy and delicious our friends would love them." Trica pleaded.

"I know where you can find some." They heard a new voice say from behind a tree.

Trica and Stego both jumped.

"Who's there?" Stego spoke bravely to the new voice.

A tall, strange looking dinosaur walked out from behind the tree. He walked on two feet, had long claws at the end of his hands, and sharp teeth peeking from his mouth. He looked a little scary to Trica and Stego.

"Hello there, my name is Rex." The new dinosaur spoke softly. "I know I look a little scary, but please don't be afraid of me. All I want is a friend but everyone runs away from me."

Trica and Stego saw how sad Rex looked. They both said hello to the new dinosaur, as they both knew better than to be afraid of new things.

"My name is Stego and this is Trica, it's lovely to meet you."

"It's sad that people keep running away from you, but we won't." Trica smiled at him. "You said you know where to find oranges?"

"Yes! We can find them just up ahead near the meadow." Rex said excitedly.

"That's perfect!" Stego jumped up and down. "Rex, would you like to come help us get oranges? Then you can join us and our friends for a picnic."

Rex was so excited to have new friends he could barely contain himself. A big smile came across his face as he shouted, "I would love that!"

Rex took up a piece of the giant leaf to help Trica and Stego drag it. The three dinosaurs collected enough oranges to fill the leaf. They then made their way to the meadow. Trica and Stego were excited to introduce their new friend to everyone. They found their friends playing in the meadow. They walked up to them together, but when everyone saw Rex they screamed and ran away.

This made Rex sad and he frowned. They all knew Trica and Stego were friendly dinosaurs, but Rex looked new and frightening to them. They ran away from him, but Trica and Stego called after them.

"Wait everyone! Please don't be afraid!" Trica cried out. "This is Rex and he is our new friend."

All their friends stopped running, screaming, and came out from their hiding places.

"Rex is so friendly and all he wants is friends," Stego explained. "He looks new and different, but that doesn't mean we should judge him on that. We should get to know him first."

Their friends all looked at each other and felt bad. They had run away from the new dinosaur without even giving him a chance. They were scared because he was new and different. They didn't know what to expect, so they were afraid.

The creatures all came up to Rex slowly and apologized for running away like they had. They shouldn't have been scared of him just because he was new. They all introduced themselves and Rex couldn't be happier. He finally had some friends.

Trica looked at all her friends and said "See, just 'cause someone or something is new and different, doesn't mean you should be afraid."

The three dinosaurs and all their friends ate the delicious food they had gathered and played the rest of the day together. They were all having so much fun, but the sun had to go down today as it did every day. Trica and Stego said goodbye to their friends as they went home. Rex thanked them for not running away from him and for being his friends. They said goodbye to the new dinosaur and were glad to have him as their friend.

The two sleepy dinosaurs walked back home and went straight to bed. They dreamed of what tomorrow's adventure would be.

The Sleepy Dinosaurs and the Patient Tortoise

Trica and Stego were walking through the forest looking for their adventure for that day. They weren't sure what would happen to them on their adventures, but they knew they would always have fun as long as they were together.

Stego and Trica always learned something during their adventures. Then they would teach their friends what they had learned. They knew they still had many more things to learn.

"Why don't we go find some star flowers near the pond?" Stego suggested as they sat in the shade.

Trica's eyes lit up. She loved to pick flowers so she could sniff them. She loved the colors and how beautiful they were.

"I think that's a great idea. Let's go!" Trica was so excited she got up and ran for the pond.

"Wait for me!" Stego cried out as he got up and ran after her.

Trica was running so fast that she didn't notice a rock-like object laying in the grass right in front of her. She ran right into the rock and tripped over it.

"Ouch!" She yelled as she fell and rolled into the grass. "I really have to stop tripping over things." She said to herself. As she looked around, she saw that the rock she tripped over wasn't a rock at all.

She looked at the mysterious object and jumped back as a head suddenly popped out of a hole in the strange rock. Then, two legs on either side slowly popped out. The creature was brown, with a rock-like shell that had beautiful patterns. It moved really slowly, almost like it was still young and didn't know how to use its legs.

Then a calm voice came from the strange rock. "Hello young dinosaur, are you okay?"

"Hello," Trica was surprised to hear the rock talk but she was too polite not to respond. "I'm sorry I tripped over you."

Stego came running in. He finally managed to catch up with Trica. He saw that she had fallen.

"Trica, are you okay?" he asked her.

As he approached her, he noticed the strange creature on the ground.

"I'm okay Stego," Trica said to her friend. "Look who I found!" She was excited to show him the beautiful creature.

"Hi, my name is Tori. It is lovely to meet you both, forgive me for being so slow." Their new friend spoke slowly and kindly. "I'm a tortoise and this is how my kind moves. After living for 50 years, I've learned that being patient and learning to wait is important."

Trica was so fascinated by the new creature. She had never seen anything like him before.

"You're 50 years old? You must have had many adventures and learned many things." Trica spoke to him. "I really am sorry for tripping over you. I was excited to pick the flowers."

Tori looked up slowly at her, and quietly said. "That's okay young dinosaur, my shell is hard as a rock. May I ask why you want to pick the flowers?"

"I love to smell them and they're pretty. The ones at the pond are my favorite." Trica explained.

"If you truly love the flowers, why do you pick them?" Tori asked in his wise voice.

Trica and Stego shared a surprised glance. They didn't understand Tori, or what he was trying to tell them.

"Why wouldn't she pick the flowers?" Stego asked him. "If she picks them, then she can walk around with them all day and smell them."

"Yes, you can," Tori agreed, "but once you pick the flower it will lose all its life. The smell will go away, and it won't look beautiful anymore. The flower will die." Hearing this made Stego and Trica sad. They had never thought of it that way. "If you wait until the sun sets then the flowers will bloom, and their smell will fill the air, and they will be more beautiful than ever. If you pick them you will only be able to smell them for a day, but if you leave them be then they may live to bloom again tomorrow and you can visit them every day."

Trica and Stego never knew that the flowers bloomed just before sunset, they would always just pick the flowers and move on.

"Stay with me here until the flowers bloom," Tori suggested. "Do not pick them this time. Be patient and wait for them to bloom today."

The two dinosaurs agreed to not pick the flowers today but rather wait to see what the tortoise had to show them. They sat there and spoke with the kind tortoise all day as they waited for the sun to set. Finally the sun began to set and each of the flowers opened slowly.

The petals unfolded to reveal a beautiful brightness that Trica and Stego had never seen before. The sweetest smell filled the air as the flowers opened. Trica couldn't believe the amount of color the flowers had. She was so happy to see it and she promised she would never pick another flower again. She would rather be patient and wait to watch them bloom, for she had never seen anything as beautiful.

"Thank you for showing us this, Tori." Trica said.

"It is my pleasure young dinosaurs." Tori spoke slowly and smiled.

They sat for a while and watched the flowers some more, but it was getting too dark and the dinosaurs were getting sleepy. They said goodbye to Tori and asked if they could come watch the flowers bloom with him again. He agreed but said they must be patient. He moves really slowly and it will take him a while to come back to the pond after he leaves it. They agreed with their new friend and promised they would always be patient.

The two sleepy dinosaurs walked back home and went straight to bed. They dreamed of what tomorrow's adventure would be.

The Sleepy Dinosaurs and the Beaver

Stego and Trica had just woken up to singing birds as the sun started to rise. It was early in the morning so the older dinosaurs weren't awake yet.

The two dinosaurs had a special adventure planned for today. They were going to walk all the way to the waterfall and collect some grapes. It was a far walk to the waterfall but it had been so long since they had eaten grapes. It would take them all day to get there and back but it was worth it.

Trica and Stego both yawned and got out of bed.

"Are you ready for our adventure today?" Stego asked Trica while she was still yawning.

"Are you sure we can't sleep a little longer?" Trica wasn't good at waking up.

"Come on Trica, you know we have a long way to walk if we want to be able to make it back before dark." Stego reminded her. "Let's go pick some strawberries for breakfast and get going?" Stego knew that Trica wouldn't be able to resist strawberries.

Trica jumped out of bed excitedly, "Okay I'm up, I'm up!"

The two dinosaurs went to pick strawberries and off they went to the waterfall. It was quite a long walk so they decided to play I spy to pass the time. They walked for ages and they played.

"I spy with my little eye something beginning with G!" Stego said, making sure not to look at it.

"Do I get a clue? I can never guess what you choose." Trica said, not feeling excited about the game.

"I picked a really easy one this time. The clue is it's green." Stego knew that Trica wasn't that good at guessing, but he just wanted to help her learn and this was a fun way.

"Hmmm, is it grass?" Trica asked hopefully.

"You got it! See, it wasn't that hard." Stego cheered.

"Okay, it wasn't that hard, but can we please play another game? I feel like we've been playing this forever." Trica was confident she could convince Stego to a race. At least then they would get to the grapes faster.

"It looks like we don't have to." Stego said as he looked ahead.

They could see the beautiful water crashing down. They had finally made it to the waterfall.

"Look Trica, we're here!" Stego shouted as he ran toward the water.

"Yay!" Trica ran after Stego.

The two dinosaurs were happy to have finally made it. They ran all the way to the bottom of the fountain where the grape vines wrapped and weaved themselves all along the stone walls surrounding the water. They picked as many grapes as they could eat and then they laid down on the grass for a nap before their walk back.

Before Trica could fall asleep, she heard a loud banging, as if something was smacking a tree somewhere nearby. She looked all around her to try to spot what was making the sound. She saw some kind of creature in the middle of the river ahead.

It was a strange furry creature with a large flat tail. It looked like it was building something. As she looked closer, she saw even more of these creatures building something else further down the river.

"Stego look at this!" She called to her friend. "There are creatures building something in the water."

"Oh wow, let's go and check it out."

Stego and Trica got up and moved toward the one creature all by himself. He was the closest one to them and they were still tired from their walk.

They came just to the start of the water and walked in. Trica loved to swim and Stego wasn't against having a bath. As they came to the strange creature he introduced himself as soon as he saw them.

"Oh my, hello, my name is Bob. What are you two doing swimming through the water?" The beaver asked them kindly. He seemed nervous but excited to meet the dinosaurs.

"Hi, my name is Stego."

"And I'm Trica. We saw you all the way out here by yourself and we were wondering what you were doing?" Trica and Stego gave the nervous creature their biggest smiles.

"I am trying to build my home, but as you said, I am all alone and it's a difficult job for one." Bob answered them with a frown.

Trica and Stego looked at him, confused. They wondered why the little beaver was all alone while there were many more beavers further down the river.

"Why don't you ask the beavers over there for help with your house?" Trica asked.

"I wanted to do it by myself, so I left those beavers to try." Bob explained. "I don't think I can go ask them for help after I said I could do it all alone." He hung his head down in sadness.

"I think you should still try and ask for help," Trica suggested.

"Yes! Come with us and we will help you ask the other beavers for help." Stego tried to encourage the beaver.

Bob thought about it for a moment, "Okay, I'll come with you." He agreed.

They walked to the other beavers with Bob on Trica's back. As they came to the other beavers they all shouted "Hello!" to their old friend Bob. They had missed him a lot since he left.

"Hello little beavers." Trica said kindly. "Bob was afraid to admit to you that he had made a mistake. He could really use some help building his house. Do you think you could all find it in your hearts to help him?"

The beavers didn't hesitate. They all cheered and jumped for joy. One of them ran up to Bob and helped him down from Trica's back.

"We would love to help you Bob," the beaver said. "We're sorry you couldn't do it by yourself but we'll always be here to help you no matter what!"

"Really?" Bob asked with a tear coming down his cheek. "Thank you guys, I'm sorry I ran off. I guess there are just some things that you can't do alone."

"Oh Bob," Stego giggled. "It's okay if there are things you can't do by yourself and it's okay to ask for help. Everyone needs help sometimes."

Trica smiled at her friend then looked at the beaver. "I know it's hard to admit when you've made a mistake but you can't be ashamed of it. Admitting to our mistakes is what helps us learn from them and we must never feel afraid to ask for help or help others."

"We would love to stay and help but we should get going." Stego said as he looked up at the setting sun. "We need to get home before it gets too dark."

Bob hugged his beaver friends and then they all waved goodbye to the two sleepy dinosaurs. They had a long walk back home but they played some games on the way which tired them out further.

The two sleepy dinosaurs walked back home and went straight to bed. They dreamed of what tomorrow's adventure would be.

The Sleepy Dinosaurs and the Fireflies

Trica and Stego had so much fun with each other but they also loved to visit their friends. One day they went to visit their friends, the mice. They gathered oranges and berries for their friends on the way to see them. They ran and played all day, they didn't want the day to end. They chased the mice through the meadow. They went swimming after eating their fruit. They played many games and had so much fun.

Trica and Stego were always going on adventures and making sure they got home before dark. Today the two dinosaurs didn't realize how late they had been playing with their friends. They had been so caught up chasing and playing with the mice that when they looked around, they saw that the sun had already set and the night was all around them.

"Oh no Stego," Trica gasped. "It's dark already and we have no way of seeing our way home. Our parents are going to be worried about us." Trica was very frightened.

"Don't worry Trica," Stego said calmly. "I'm sure we'll be able to find a way home. We just need something to light our way."

The mice felt bad for their friends. They had forgotten that they needed to be home before the sun set and now they were stuck out here in the dark.

"I know who could help!" Spoke one of the mice. "Maybe the fireflies will help light your way home. They are very kind and love to help those who ask. I will go find them." With that the little mouse jumped off.

The two dinosaurs stayed with the other mice as they waited. It was getting darker the longer they waited. Trica was even more scared now and so was Stego. Suddenly a single light appeared out of the dark and spoke to the two dinosaurs.

"Hello, I am the queen of the fireflies. I have no name, so you can call me Queen." Stego and Trica looked up at the tiny, floating light as it came down to them. "You two look scared. What is wrong?"

"We stayed out too late and we can't find our way home." Stego explained to the queen while holding on to Trica.

"Do you think you can show us the way?" Trica asked, trying not to sound as scared as she was.

"I would like to help, but first you must first speak the magic words." The queen told them and waited patiently to hear those words.

"What magic words? We don't know the magic words. Are you able to help us get home or not?" Trica asked Queen Firefly stubbornly. Trica was very scared and not thinking properly. As she spoke, the firefly's light grew dim and she frowned.

The firefly repeated herself. "I would like to help, however you must first speak the magic words." She waited patiently as she did the last time.

The two dinosaurs were very confused. They weren't sure what the firefly meant. Each time they asked, the firefly's light would dim more and more, until the light was nearly gone.

Trica was so afraid she pleaded one last time to the firefly. "Please Queen Firefly, can you please help us find our way home!"

The queen smiled for that was the word she was waiting for. As Trica spoke the word, a group of lights appeared one by one lighting a path through the forest. Each light was so bright they seemed to outshine the moon.

"The lights will now lead you home," the queen told Trica and Stego. "The first magic word was please, which you have spoken. You must make sure to say the two remaining magic words or my fireflies will not help you again."

Trica and Stego stood up, enchanted by the bright light of the fireflies. Trica smiled up at the queen.

"Thank you," she spoke softly. "Those are the last magic words, aren't they?"

The queen nodded her head, "No matter how you're feeling, whether you are angry or scared, you should always be good mannered and thank those who are helping you. Please and thank you are the magic words that will always help you in times of need."

The two dinosaurs understood what the firefly had tried to teach them

"Thank you, Queen Firefly, we will always remember to say please and thank you, no matter what." Stego told her.

They followed the light of the fireflies as they led them through the forest in the dark. They weren't scared anymore because they knew they would be safe. They made sure to say thank you to every firefly they passed.

The two sleepy dinosaurs made it home and went straight to bed. They dreamed of what tomorrow's adventure would be.

The Sleepy Dinosaurs and the Different Bee

One day Trica and Stego were exploring a new part of the woods they had never been in before. They were trying to find new places with food for them and their friends. They had made so many new friends lately and the two dinosaurs loved to have picnics. But the more friends they made, the more food they had to find.

The two dinosaurs were searching all day for some kind of delicious new treat they could give their friends. They looked all over but they had no luck.

"I don't know if we'll be able to find a new treat today, Stego." Trica said as she was searching through some bushes.

"But we're having a picnic tomorrow and it would be so nice to have something new to give our friends." Stego was determined and he wouldn't give up. "We still have plenty of time before we have to go back home."

"Okay, we can look a little longer. Maybe we just need to walk a little further into the forest!" Trica suggested hopefully.

They walked and searched high and low for their new treat, whatever it might be. They search late into the day. Trica and Stego were just about to give up when they reached a small valley filled with beautiful and tall purple flowers.

The valley was filled with flowers but what really caught their eye was a strange looking cocoon hanging from a low branch in the middle of the valley. There were swarms of little black and yellow flying creatures around the cocoon. As they walked closer, they noticed one of the little insects flying off to a rock nearby.

Trica and Stego decided to follow the little creature. They came closer to it and they could hear a soft cry coming from the rock.

Trica and Stego weren't sure what was wrong, but they couldn't stand to hear anyone cry.

"What's wrong little guy?" Stego asked as they approached the little creature laying on the rock.

The black and yellow creature looked up at the two dinosaurs and wiped his tears away. "I'm sad," He sniffled. "I'm sad because all the other bees are the same and I'm different."

"How are you different?" Trica asked. She looked at the little bee and then looked back at the ones flying around the valley. She didn't see any difference.

The bee sniffed again. "You see, I have black and yellow stripes, but they all have yellow and black stripes. They all make a buzzing sound, but I make a humming sound." The bee started to cry again. "I'm afraid if they see I'm different from them then they won't like me."

The two dinosaurs couldn't believe what they had just heard. Stego felt angry that the poor bee felt this way. He stayed calm enough to talk some sense into the little bee.

"No one should be afraid to be themselves," Stego told him. "You are who you are, and no one can change that. You're amazing just the way you are and it's okay if you're not the same as everyone else. It's good to be different because that's who you are."

"Yeah, why should it matter what color your stripes are?" Trica added. "If you are a good bee, and a good friend then it shouldn't matter what you look like."

The bee sniffed one last time and looked up at them, "So, I shouldn't care if I'm not like everyone else? As long as I am friendly and nice, then people will like me?" The bee asked the two dinosaurs hopefully.

"Exactly!" Trica jumped up excitedly. "If you be yourself then the people who deserve to be your friends will like you. If they don't like you then they aren't your friends."

"Always remember to be yourself," Stego added with a smile.

The bee stood up and smiled brightly. He flapped his tiny wings and flew up high in the air with excitement. Trica and Stego had made him so happy with what they had told him. He was ready to go back to the other bees with his new-found confidence.

"Thank you so much my new friends, I will never forget what you've taught me today." The little bee told them before flying to rejoin the other bees.

"It's our pleasure," Stego called after him before turning to Trica. "It's too bad we still haven't found something new to eat."

The bee flew back to them after hearing what Stego said.

"Something to eat?" He asked. "I normally just eat my family's delicious honey. We make it ourselves using the pollen from these beautiful flowers." The bee explained to Trica and Stego.

"Honey?" Trica thought for a moment. "I don't think we've tried that before."

"Would you like me to get you some?" The bee kindly offered. "It really is very delicious!"

"We would love to try some." Stego cried out excitedly.

The bee went high up into the tree and grabbed a large leaf and flew toward his home. Trica and Stego waited for him by the rock. In a few moments the bee flew out of his home with a leaf filled with yellow, gooey honey.

The dinosaurs were so excited that they jumped and cheered for the bee. They tried a drop of the honey as soon as possible.

"It's so sweet and sticky!" Trica shouted in excitement.

"It really is amazing!" Stego agreed with Trica. "Our friends are going to love to try this, thank you so much little bee."

The two dinosaurs were so happy to have met their new friend the bee, but it had started to get dark. They thanked the little bee for the honey and said goodbye to him. They carried the leaf filled with honey home and couldn't wait to share it with their friends at the picnic. They needed to get a lot of sleep that night, so they were ready for their big day.

The two sleepy dinosaurs walked back home and went straight to bed. They dreamed of what tomorrow's adventure would be.

If you enjoyed this book in anyway, an honest review is always appreciated!

CPSIA information can be obtained
at www.ICGtesting.com
Printed in the USA
LVHW080947130522
718708LV00010B/113